Chip & Cookie

The First Adventure

High on Ice Cream Mountain, nestled in a magical forest, stands the tiny village of Raspberry Swirl. Just beyond the root beer fountain lives Grandma Dovely in a cozy white cottage. Red geraniums and green ivy spill from the window boxes and red hearts circle her door.

Early each morning Grandma Dovely baked treats for the villagers — high loaves of wheat bread, plump corn muffins, scrumptious strudel, and tasty turnovers. Every afternoon, the village children came to help Grandma Dovely bake chocolate chip cookies. Together they mixed the ingredients and baked the cookies until they were golden brown. Then Grandma Dovely and the children munched the still-warm-from-the-oven cookies in the garden as they laughed and talked and told each other stories.

Grandma Dovely often said, "I'm so glad you're here. What a happy family we are. Sharing cookies is like sharing love. The more you give away, the happier you feel."

One afternoon Grandma Dovely sat in her rocker, staring sadly at her chocolate chip cookie recipe.

"Creampuff," she said to her furry kitten friend, "I don't understand it. Sultan Semi-sweet has suddenly stopped sending me chocolate chips and we can't bake cookies without them."

Creampuff washed his whiskers and purred thoughtfully. "No chocolate chip cookies?" he said. "The children will come and if there is no baking party, they will be sad."

Grandma Dovely jumped up and opened her sewing basket. "We'll have our afternoon party," she cried, "with a wonderful surprise for the children."

Grandma Dovely cut pieces of dark brown fabric into the shapes of chocolate chips and sewed them onto two big round circles of cloth. When she stitched smiling faces onto the cloth cookies and added arms and legs, Creampuff stopped washing his whiskers.

"Those are not ordinary cookies," he said.

"They're dolls," said Grandma Dovely. "They're chocolate chip cookie dolls!" Grandma Dovely made bright blue shoes for her cookie dolls and, just for fun, decorated each shoe with stars. She made a cap for the boy doll and a purse for the girl doll and kissed each doll right on its pink heart nose.

Magically, as if they were baking, the dolls plumped up and up until their toes danced in their bright blue shoes and their dark eyes glittered, and the room filled with the delicious smells of cookies baking.

"I'm Chip," said the boy cookie as he jumped to his feet and petted Creampuff's soft fur.

"My name is Cookie," said the girl cookie and she gave Grandma Dovely a big hug.

That afternoon when the children arrived at the bakery, they had more fun than ever. They played games with Chip and Cookie: hopscotch and marbles and hide-and-go-seek. They laughed and danced and shared their secrets. Chip and Cookie hugged each child and promised to be their friends forever.

But the next day Grandma Dovely sat sadly in her rocker again. Still no chocolate chips from Sultan Semi-sweet.

"Why don't you go to the Sultan's palace and get them yourself?" asked Cookie.

"I would go if I could," said Grandma Dovely, "Sultan Semi-sweet's chocolate palace is on the other side of the Brown Sugar Desert, much too far for me to travel."

"We'll go!" sang Chip and Cookie, their brown eyes full of love.

"Oh, thank you," said Grandma Dovely. She gave them a map which Cookie tucked carefully into her purse.

J ust before Grandma Dovely kissed them good-bye, she plucked sixteen red hearts from her doorway and pasted four each on their bright blue shoes.

"These hearts are from my heart and their magic is love," she told them. "Now if you are in trouble, remember that your friends love you and be brave."

Chip and Cookie slid down Ice Cream Mountain, hiked across Peanut Butter Valley, and rode the peppermint stick ferry boat across Vanilla Pond.

They stepped out of the boat into Buttercup Meadow. There they met sorrowful Sally sitting in a clump of gloomy gooseberry bushes.

"It's sad, so sad," cried Sally.

"So sad," honked the gooseberries.

"What's sad?" asked Chip.

"No more chocolate chip cookies," sobbed Sally. "Nothing will ever be good again."

"Why not?" said Chip. "And what are you doing to find out why Sultan Semi-sweet stopped sending chocolate chips?"

"Do!?" asked the gooseberries. "What can we do? We're too sad to do anything. Without chocolate chip cookies life is so sad, so sad."

"You silly gooseberries," said Cookie. "It does no good to cry about your problems. We're going to find the Sultan and help Grandma Dovely bake her cookies again."

Cookie plucked one of the hearts from her shoe and gave it to Sally.

"This heart is from our hearts," said Cookie. "Its magic is love. Whenever you are sad, remember that your friends love you and be happy."

Sally and the gooseberries stopped crying and smiled.

Chip and Cookie looked at their map and then followed a winding path through a grove of pecan trees. As they hurried around a curve, they bumped smack into a white-haired man with a cane in one hand and a tiny tree and a shovel in the other. The man stumbled and plopped down right in the middle of the path.

"Excuse me," said Chip, helping the man up.

"Are you hurt?" asked Cookie, gathering up the cane, the tree, and the shovel.

To their surprise the man said, "Thank you, thank you. I'm Professor McNutt and I'm so glad you bumped into me!"

"**W**hy?" asked Chip.

"This is the best thing that's happened to me since the Magic Tree Fairy visited me," said the old man. "I live here alone and I'm very lonely with no one to talk to. Come on, bump into me again."

"Why do you stay here if you're lonely?" asked Cookie.

"The Magic Tree Fairy gave me trees that grow perfect pecans, and I must take care of them," he said. "I'm on my way now to find the right spot to plant this little tree. When I do, it will grow the best pecans you've ever tasted."

"Yum," said Chip.

"Double yum," said Cookie.

"Stay with me," said the professor. "You can be my helpers. I need someone to talk to."

"We can't stay," said Chip, "We've promised to find Sultan Semi-sweet and get chocolate chips for Grandma Dovely. But on our way back, we'll help you find a home for the little pecan tree."

"And we'll give you a present now," Cookie said.

Chip took a heart off his shoe. "This heart is from our hearts. Its magic is love. Whenever you are lonely, remember that your friends love you."

Professor McNutt tucked the heart into his shirt pocket.

"Thank you," he said. "I feel less lonely already."

Chip and Cookie set off again in search of Sultan Semi-sweet. At the edge of the Brown Sugar Desert, they stopped to catch their breath. Dunes of brown sugar stretched as far they could see.

"The Sultan's palace is farther than I thought it would be," said Cookie. "I'm tired."

"So am I," said Chip. "And my feet hurt."

They sat down to rest. As Cookie rubbed her aching feet, she touched one of the hearts that Grandma Dovely had put on her shoes and she didn't feel nearly so tired.

"Look at your shoes," she told Chip.

He looked. He smiled at Cookie and said, "We're having an adventure."

"And love will help us through all our troubles," she said. "Even aching feet."

"Come on, Cookie," Chip said, as he jumped up, "Grandma Dovely is depending on us."

The Sultan's palace appeared on the horizon. Milk chocolate turrets rose far above them. Dark chocolate domes and white chocolate towers brushed the cotton candy clouds. A bridge of sugar wafers stretched across the moat of pure melted semi-sweet chocolate. Chocolate baskets filled with strawberries and marshmallows and fat roasted peanuts lined the sides of the bridge. On each basket a sign read: "Please take a treat and dip in the moat. Eat before entering the Palace."

Chip took a marshmallow and Cookie chose a strawberry. Kneeling on the side of the bridge, they dipped their treats in the melted chocolate and ate them.

Then they knocked on the palace door.

There was no answer. They pushed open the door and went inside. It was cool in the palace, but they could hear strange rumblings and grumblings coming from somewhere. Chip and Cookie hurried from room to room, through the kitchen with its copper bowls filled with chocolate, past tall chocolate statues in the courtyard, and finally up a winding chocolate stairway.

At the top was a huge dark room. The rumblings and grumblings were coming from inside. Chip and Cookie held hands and tiptoed in. Inside, lying on a bed of chocolate-covered caramel, was Sultan Semi-sweet, rumbling and grumbling and snoring in his sleep.

Chip and Cookie edged closer. "Can you hear me?" Cookie whispered.

The Sultan's eyes popped open. "Do I look like a fence post?" he bellowed.

"No," said Cookie, frightened by his response. "You look like Sultan Semi-sweet."

"Can you walk?" asked Chip, again being polite.

"Of course I can walk," screamed the Sultan. "Do I look like a goldfish?"

"Then why don't you get up?" asked Cookie.

"Because I'm stuck in my bed and I don't want to," shouted the Sultan. "All I do is deliver chocolate chips and no one ever invites me to their baking parties. I'm sick and tired of being left out."

Chip and Cookie said with alarm, "We know the children will share their cookies with you, but you must supply Grandma Dovely with the chocolate chips to make them."

"No," sulked the Sultan. "I'm going to keep them all to myself."

Chip and Cookie looked at each other. Then Cookie reached for a red heart from her bright blue shoes. "This heart is from our hearts," she said shyly. "It's an invitation to be part of our hearts and our parties forever. Whenever you feel mean and left out, remember that your friends love you and be sweet and friendly again."

"Sweet, sweet. Do I look like a chocolate chip?" asked the Sultan, his anger disappearing.

"Yes!" said Chip and Cookie with delight.

Chip and Cookie opened the windows and the warm air softened the Sultan's chocolate-covered caramel bed so he could get up.

"Now that I'm free and sweet, so sweet again, let's take Grandma Dovely her chocolate chips," said the Sultan as he put the red heart in his pocket. From his pantry he took two giant watermelon shells. He added donut wheels and candy cane handles, and made two wheelbarrows. In no time at all, Chip and Cookie had filled the wheelbarrows to overflowing and pushed them into the Sultan's magic chariot. Then pulled by his prancing chocolate horses, they set out for Ice Cream Mountain.

On the way, they picked up Professor McNutt and his little pecan tree and Sally and her gooseberries. Flying through the cotton candy clouds in the magic chariot, they all sang:

> We're glad, so glad to be together.

> We're glad, so glad to share together.

> We're glad, so glad to love each other.

> Life is fun with friends to love.

When they reached Ice Cream Mountain, the Sultan looked for a shady place to park his tired horses, and Chip and Cookie pushed the overflowing wheelbarrows proudly up to Grandma Dovely's door. The door burst open and Grandma Dovely rushed out to kiss them, while the children hugged them and Creampuff wound himself around their ankles and purred. Everyone was glad to see Chip and Cookie safely home and to meet their new friends Professor McNutt, Sally, and the gooseberries.

"Thank you for finding the Sultan and bringing home the chocolate chips," Grandma Dovely said to Chip and Cookie. "Did you have a hard trip?"

"We had an adventure," said Chip, and he winked at Cookie.

Grandma Dovely peered at their shoes. "You lost three of your hearts," she said.

"Oh, we didn't lose them," said Chip. "We gave them to our new friends."

"Good," said Grandma Dovely, and she took three new red hearts from the bakery door and put them on their bright blue shoes. "Hearts are like cookies; they are meant to be shared."

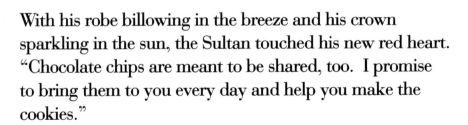

Professor McNutt, wearing the heart Chip had given him, said, "Trees need to grow in places filled with love. Pecans are meant to be shared." And he planted his little tree right then and there in Grandma Dovely's garden, so she would always have perfect pecans for her cookies.

With his robe billowing in the breeze and his crown sparkling in the sun, the Sultan touched his new red heart. "Chocolate chips are meant to be shared, too. I promise to bring them to you every day and help you make the cookies."

"We're glad, so glad," sang sunny Sally and the gooseberries.

"Let's bake!" shouted the children.

When the chocolate chip cookies were golden brown, Grandma Dovely took them out of the oven and carried them into the garden. Chip and Cookie, Sultan Semi-sweet, Professor McNutt, Sally, the gooseberries, Grandma Dovely, and the children sat in the shade of the pecan tree and ate the warm, crunchy cookies they had made together. They laughed and talked and told each other stories. And when the stories were told and the cookies were eaten, they all sang together:

We're glad, so glad to be together.

We're glad, so glad to share together.

We're glad, so glad to love each other.

Life is fun with friends to love.

When they shared their hearts and their love — and their chocolate chip cookies — they were never sad, lonely or angry again.

Grandma Dovely's
Chocolate Chip Cookie Recipe

Preheat oven to 375 degrees

Cream and blend together:
2 sticks (1 cup) soft butter from Buttercup Meadow
3/4 cup brown sugar from Brown Sugar Desert
3/4 cup white sugar
2 eggs
1 tsp. vanilla extract from Vanilla Pond

Sift and stir in:
2-1/2 cups all purpose flour
1 tsp. baking soda
1/2 tsp. salt

Add:
2 cups of the Sultan's semi-sweet chocolate chips
3/4 cup of Professor McNutt's pecans, sliced

Drop the batter from a teaspoon onto a cookie sheet,
leaving lots of room in between each cookie. Bake for
about 10 minutes, or until the cookies are as brown as you
wish. Serve with milk or juice and share with friends.

ACROPOLIS BOOKS, LTD.
In Metropolitan Washington since 1958
13950 Park Center Road
Herndon, VA 22071

Attention: Schools and Corporations
ACROPOLIS books are available at quan-
tity discounts with bulk purchase for educa-
tional, business, or sales promotional use.

For information, please write to:

SPECIAL SALES DEPARTMENT,
ACROPOLIS BOOKS, LTD.,
13950 Park Center Road
Herndon, VA 22071

50¢ from the sale of each copy of *Wally
Amos Presents CHIP & COOKIE* will
be donated to:
Literacy Volunteers of America
5795 Widewaters Parkway
Syracuse, NY 13214

**Library of Congress
Cataloging-in-Publication Data**

Kehret, Peg.
Wally Amos presents Chip & Cookie: the
first adventure created by Christine Harris-
Amos / story by Peg Kehret; illustrated by
Leslie Beaber.
p.   cm.
Summary: On their journey across the
Brown Sugar Desert to get chocolate chips
from Sultan Semi-Sweet, two cookie dolls
teach those they meet about the magic of
love.
ISBN 0-87491-988-6: $14.95

[1. Chocolate chip cookies—Fiction. 2.,
Love—Fiction. 3. Dolls—Fiction.] I.
Beaber, Leslie, ill. II. Title. III. Title: Wally
Amos presents Chip and Cookie.
PZ7.K2518Wal   1991
[E]—dc20   91-29047
                                           CIP
                                            AC